The Computer Teacher
from the
Black Lagoon

by Mike Thaler · pictures by Jared Lee

SCHOLASTIC INC.

New York   Toronto   London   Auckland   Sydney
Mexico City   New Delhi   Hong Kong   Buenos Aires

visit us at www.abdopublishing.com

Reinforced library bound edition published in 2012 by Spotlight,
a division of the ABDO Group, PO Box 398166, Minneapolis, MN 55439. Spotlight produces high-quality
reinforced library bound editions for schools and libraries. Published by agreement with Scholastic Inc.

Printed in the United States of America, North Mankato, Minnesota.
102011
122012

 This book contains at least 10% recycled materials.

To Dr. Illo,
who puts my back on line.
—M.T.

To 2LT Fred Szabo
—SP/4 Lee

Library of Congress Cataloging-in-Publication Data

This book was previously cataloged with the following information:
Thaler, Mike, 1936-
  The computer teacher from the Black Lagoon / by Mike Thaler ; pictures by Jared Lee.
    p.   cm.
Summary: A boy contemplates all the horrible stories he has heard about the computer teacher, Miss Pluggins,
and the ordeals she forces her students to endure.
[1. Teachers —Juvenile fiction. 2. Computers —Juvenile fiction. 3. Schools —Juvenile Fiction.]
PZ7.T3 Com 2007
[E}-dc22
                                        2008297277
ISBN 978-1-59961-955-2 (reinforced library edition)

All Spotlight books are reinforced library bindings
and manufactured in the United States of America.

I have to take a computer class this year.

The teacher is Miss Pluggins.

The kids say she has an electric personality, a good memory,
and drives you very hard.

She also has a lot of energy, and is always looking for an outlet.

She lives in a lab with a herd of one-eyed monitors that stare at you all day.

She also has a big dog, named Browser, that won't let you escape.

She locks you in a keypad, sets you in the backspace, and boots you up.

Then she puts you on the *Weird Wild Web* where you have
to go surfing with a mouse.

I hope the weird wild spider doesn't get us.

In each class, she makes one kid enter a computer to find out how many bites it has.

When it's done, there are just shoelaces left.

Everything the computer eats goes on a menu.

SALSA

I heard Miss Pluggins just eats disks and chips.

The computer can also cast a spell on you.

I heard it has a *spell hex* and a *cursor* that can turn you into a frog and file you away. ZIP!

And watch out for the *pixels*!

They tie you onto a log and ram information into your head.

It's called *downloading*, and you just might wind up as roadkill on the information superhighway.

Eric says you can also get run-over by a search engine or flattened when the computer crashes. I hope we wear seatbelts.

Then, when you're thin enough, you go on a home page, or fly into hyperlink and hang out at a space bar.

If you have pimples, you go into the zit file.

○ ←PIMPLE
◎ ←MARBLE
◉ ←CIRCLE

You also have to look out for *The Hacker*, avoid *THE BLOG*, and don't get tangled up in the Internet.

The computer can also catch a virus. Will we have to get shots from the nurse?

Eric says his dad got hung up online for months, developed a floppy disc, and can't stand up anymore.

It all sounds very dangerous to me. Well, here we go.

We march into the computer lab.

They're all lined up like an army of Cyclopes just waiting for us.

I don't see Browser or the weird wild spider.

Miss Pluggins tells us we are beginning a great adventure. I know...I heard.

She says we will be able to access all the information in the world, talk to China in a click, make our own Valentine cards, write and illustrate our own books, and play computer games.

"Hey, let's get started! Where's that mouse?"